THE ADVENTURES OF THE EARTH SAVER GIRL

Don't Be A Litterbug

By Brooklyn
Illustrated by Zhu Hui Hui

WRIGHT
BOOK PUBLISHING

The Adventures of the Earth Saver Girl
Copyright © 2010 by Wright Book Publishing
All rights reserved.

ISBN 978-0-9822822-4-3

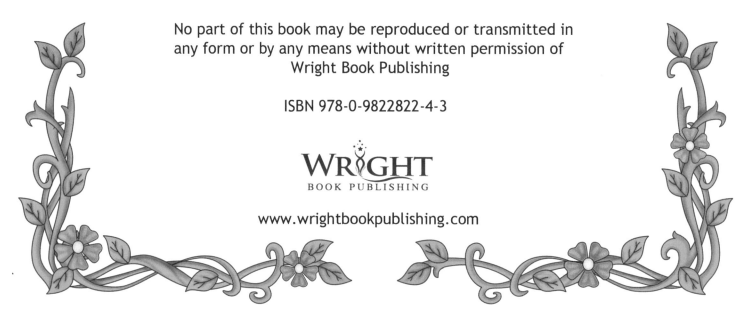

WRIGHT
BOOK PUBLISHING

www.wrightbookpublishing.com

Layla and her mother Joan Kendricks had the prettiest yard in the neighborhood. It was full of beautiful flowers, a gazebo and a huge treehouse. Layla's mother told her how her father built the treehouse with recycled materials from a scrap yard.

On Layla's 9th birthday she played in her treehouse as she did almost every day. She spotted a red flashing button. "Where did that come from?" wondered Layla. She slowly walked towards the button. She stared at it trying to get up the courage to press it. She pressed the button and said FIYA! Layla always said fiya when she was about to do something fun or exciting. Her treehouse changed. It had computerized maps, monitors and buttons everywhere. "Wow!" shouted Layla.

She heard a voice say "FIYA!" She looked around to see who said it. On a monitor appeared her father. "Happy birthday baby girl," said her father. Layla stared at the monitor. She was shocked to see her daddy. Her father continued, "I'm sorry I couldn't be there on your birthday but I have been waiting for you to turn nine so I can tell you a very important secret." Layla continued to stare at the monitor.

"Get your litter getter stick and tap it on the floor two times then say FIYA!" said her father. Layla's litter getter is a tool she uses to pick up trash so she doesn't have to touch the trash with her hands. Layla looked around her treehouse and found her litter getter stick. She picked it up and slowly tapped it twice. "FIYA!" shouted Layla. Layla's clothes changed from her shorts and shirt to a superhero outfit. "You are now old enough to help me rid the earth of trash and pollution. You are now The Earth Saver Girl!" said her father.

Layla spent the next few weeks in her lab learning about litter and how bad it is for the earth. She also monitored her communities' biggest litterbugs. When a person litters too much their name would light up on her map. "Let's see this week's culprit," said Layla. She pressed a button and a very surprising name and face appeared. "Morgan Martin? My very own cousin is this week's biggest litterbug? His littering has got to stop!"

"Layla!" her mother yelled up to her treehouse. Layla did not hear her. Layla's mother yelled once more, but Layla still did not hear her. Her mother climbed up the ladder and knocked on the door. Layla quickly pushed a button that changed her lab back into a regular treehouse. Layla's mother waited patiently as Layla made it to the door.

"Yes, Mommy," Layla answered as she opened the door. "What do you do up here? I've been calling you," said Mrs. Kendricks. "You know me, always doing something. Are you ready for our walk?" asked Layla. Everyday Layla and her Mother would walk around their neighborhood to pick up trash and to get some exercise. "Yes, we're going to meet Aunt Donna and Morgan at the park," said her mother. "Great! Morgan is just the person I want to see," said Layla as she looked around her treehouse. "Just let me get my litter getter."

As Layla and her mother walked to the park she spotted a pile of trash. "Mommy why do people throw cigarette butts on the ground?" Layla asked as she gripped them with her litter getter. "Probably because they are too lazy to find a trash can," replied her mother. "Don't they know that cigarettes are the most littered item in the world? Don't they know butts have poison inside of them that can leak into our water? Don't they know that they can start deadly fires? Don't they know it takes 5 years for them to decompose?" Layla mother stood amazed that Layla knew all that information. *Wow where did that come from?* Layla thought.

"Where did you learn all of that Layla?" asked her mother. "I've been reading," replied Layla. "The next time I see Uncle Lucas I'm gonna tell him those facts because I saw him throw a butt on the ground. Now every time I see one I see his face." Mrs. Kendricks laughed. "What's so funny mommy?" asked Layla. "You just called your uncle a butt face." Layla and her mother laughed. "I just wish people would keep their stinky butts off our streets." Mrs. Kendricks laughed harder, "stinky butts, you're so funny Layla."

Layla greeted her Aunt Donna with a big hug. "Did Uncle Lucas come?" asked Layla. "No, he's at home preparing for our cookout tonight. He said he's making your favorite chicken kabobs," replied Aunt Donna. "I love those kabobs! Where's Morgan?" asked Layla. "He's over by the skateboard ramp," replied Aunt Donna. "I should've known. Mommy may I go over there with Morgan?" asked Layla. "Yes baby, Aunt Donna and I will be right here."

Morgan's friend Cameron, who is in a wheelchair see's Layla walking towards them. "Here comes your pretty cousin," said Cameron. "I just love the way she calls me Cam. How do I look?" asked Cameron. "If you like her so much why don't you tell her?" asked Morgan. "I can't," replied Cameron. "I'm gonna tell her," replied Morgan. "You better not," demanded Cameron. "Hey Layla," Cameron said with a big smile. "Hey Cam," replied Layla.

"What's up Morgan?" asked Layla. "Nothing, just waiting for my turn to compete for a chance to meet Mason Davidson." He drinks the rest of his sports drink and throws the bottle on the ground. "Pick that up!" shouted Layla. "No way! I can't skate with it," replied Morgan. "Well pick it up and thrown it in the trash," said Layla. "Do you see a trash can around here?" asked Morgan. "Yeah there's one over there," said Layla as she pointed to the trash can.

"I'm not going way over there. Why don't you pick it up? You pick up everybody else's trash with your little litter getter," said Morgan. Layla and Morgan argued back and forth about the bottle. "Wait!" shouted Cameron. "I'll pick it up!" He rolled over, picked up the bottle and placed it in a plastic bag on the side of his chair. "Why didn't you tell me you had a trash bag?" asked Morgan. "You didn't ask," replied Cameron.

"So who is Mason Davidson, anyway?" asked Layla. Morgan was shocked, "you don't know who Mason Davidson is? He's only the best professional skateboarder in the world," replied Morgan. "No wonder I don't know him," said Layla. "If I win today I will get to meet him tomorrow at his back to school party here in the park. "I bet if he knew how much you littered here he wouldn't want to come to our park." "Well, he is and besides everybody litter's here," replied Morgan. "Not me," said Layla. "Me either," said Cameron. "Anyway it's always, magically cleaned by the next day" said Morgan. "You think it's magic?" asked Layla. "All I know is for the past few weeks the park has been cleaner than ever and there is no way three park cleaners can clean all this mess."

"Dude, did you bump your head when you fell earlier?" asked Cameron. "Are you saying you think a trash fairy comes every night and cleans the park?" laughed Cameron. *FIYA*, Layla said to herself. *I'll show him a fairy, just wait until tonight.* "Look around at all this mess," Morgan continued "there is just too much trash for them to pick up." "Yeah and you're responsible for most of it," said Layla. "How do you know? Who are you anyway, the trash monitor?" asked Morgan. "Yeah," said Layla "and I work with the trash fairy." Layla and Cameron laughed.

"Morgan Martin," a lady called over a loud speaker. "Finally it's my turn. I gotta win," said Morgan as he ran towards the skate ramp. "Good luck," shouted Layla and Cameron.

That evening everyone went to Morgan's house for the cookout. "Layla," laughed her mother, "don't you have something to talk to Uncle Lucas about?" Layla laughed. "Yes ma'am," she replied and walked over to where her uncle was cooking on the grill. "Your chicken kabobs are almost ready," said Uncle Lucas as she walked up to him at the grill. "Thank you Uncle Lucas, those are my favorite, but I wanted to talk to you about something else," said Layla. "Princess you know you can talk to me about anything," said Uncle Lucas.

Layla took a deep breath and began telling him all the dangers of littering cigarette butts. "Wow," said Uncle Lucas. "Where did you learn all of that?" he asked. "I've been studying," replied Layla. "Well, Princess that's part of our celebration today, I stopped smoking," said Uncle Lucas. "That's great!" said Layla. "But, I will make sure to tell all of my friends those facts so they will stop their littering," said Uncle Lucas. Layla gave her uncle a big hug.

Every night since Layla found out that she was the Earth Saver Girl she used her special suck and sort trash pickup machine to clean up all the litter in her community. The machine would send all the recyclable trash to the recycling center and other trash to the landfill. This night she decided to do the opposite to teach Morgan a lesson. She pressed a button and sucked up all the litter but this time she sent it all to the park. She mixed a special potion for Morgan and set out to teach him a little lesson.

In through the window went the Earth Saver Girl to cast her spell on Morgan. She waved her magic litter getter stick and said the magic words, "1, 2, 3 keep our community litter free. FIYA!"

Morgan woke up excited to get to the park. "Mom we can't be late," he shouted from bathroom. "We're waiting on you sleepy head," replied his mom. "Has Cameron made it over yet?" he asked. "I'm here," answered Cameron, "all the way from next door," laughed Cameron. Morgan rushed from the bathroom and looked around, "where's Layla?" he asked. "I thought she had to ride with us since Aunt Joan had to work." "Aunt Joan decided to take the day off just to see you meet your idol, so they are going to meet us there," said Morgan's Mother. "I bet she is going to walk to pick up trash," said Morgan. "What's wrong with that?" asked Cameron.

"Mom can you go faster? I'm gonna be late," said Morgan. "The traffic is not moving," said his mother. "Wow look at all that trash," said Cameron. "You're beginning to sound like Layla," said Morgan. Morgan looked around and said, "wow that is a lot of trash. Mom since we're close to the park can we get out and walk?" Cameron looked at the trash and said, "there's no way I can make it through that trash in my chair." Morgan looked sad because he thought he hurt Cameron's feelings. "I'm sorry, I wasn't thinking," said Morgan. "Go ahead," said Cameron, "I know how bad you want to meet Mason. "Are you sure?" asked Morgan. "Yeah, go ahead," said Cameron. Morgan jumped out the car and ran towards the park.

As Cameron got closer to the park he heard a voice over the loud speaker that sounded like Layla. "Everyone lets welcome Morgan Martin to the stage." Morgan proudly made his way to the stage. "Layla why are you dressed like that?" asked Morgan. "My name is the Earth Saver Girl, not Layla," she replied. "We want Mason!" chanted the crowd. "Mason was on his way but turned around when he saw trash everywhere," said the Earth Saver Girl. "We can thank our biggest litterbug Morgan Martin, for Mason canceling." Everyone booed and threw trash at Morgan. Morgan started turning into a litterbug. He ran away dodging all the trash that was being thrown at him. "I'm sorry, I'm sorry, I'm sorry," he cried.

"Morgan!" shouted his mother as she shook him. "Wake up, you're having a bad dream." Morgan sat up with tears in his eyes. "It was a nightmare," said Morgan. "Layla was dressed like a superhero. There was so much trash in the park that Cameron couldn't get around and Mason canceled. Layla told everyone that I was the biggest litterbug, then I started turning into a bug. Everybody booed me." Just then Layla came to Morgan's bedroom door and he screamed. "What's wrong Morgan? I just wanted to see if you were ready to go to the park," said Layla. "You're not gonna throw trash at me are you?" asked Morgan. "Why would I do that?" asked Layla.

"Mom may we walk to the park?" asked Morgan. "Sure, but you never want to walk to the park why today?" asked his mother. "I want to pick up litter along the way," said Morgan. "Wow, that must have been some dream," said his mother. "I figured you would want to pick up some litter so I brought an extra litter getter for you," said Layla. "From now on, I promise to show the earth some love, I won't be a litterbug," said Morgan. *FIYA! Layla said to herself. Mission accomplished.*

Thank you for reading about my adventures. I had to teach that Morgan a little lesson about keeping our community clean. There are so many more lesson we need to learn to protect our earth, will you do your part? Visit my website at www.earthsavergirl.com to make your pledge video, play games and much more!

SEEK & FIND

Basketball, Key, Alfred The Litterbug, Broom,
Bird, Handprint, Butterfly, Magnifying Glass
Mask, Footprint, Heart Pillow, Purple Book

Can you find the 10 differences?

CPSIA information can be obtained
at www.ICGtesting.com
Printed in the USA
BVHW02n0815050718
520682BV00007B/229/P